BIG WIG

Written and illustrated by
Colin West

WALKER BOOKS
AND SUBSIDIARIES
LONDON • BOSTON • SYDNEY

Chapter One

There once lived a giant called Big Wig. He was called Big Wig because:

a) he was big

b) he wore a wig.

Big Wig was very fussy about his wig. He kept it clean and shiny with Supershine Shampoo.

And he never left home without it on top of his big bald head.

The other giants, Burpalot, Slobberchops and Smellybeard, made rude comments as Big Wig passed by.

Big Wig tried to ignore them, but he did get embarrassed, especially if Toothy Peg was around.

You see, she was Big Wig's secret love.

One day he was wandering over the mountain-tops thinking up a poem for Toothy Peg.

All was calm, till suddenly...

A gust of wind blew off his ginger wig!

It blew over one mountain-top and then another...

Big Wig watched helplessly as it vanished into the distance. He held his hands over his hairless head in horror.

Then he sloped off home more miserable than he'd ever been in his life.

Chapter Two

Not far from the Land of Giants
was the Land of Little People.
And there on a hillside lay
Big Wig's big wig.

A shepherd boy called Jonathan was the first to spot it.

He approached the ginger thing gingerly.

He poked it and prodded it.

Then he had a thought.

Jonathan dragged the tangled heap of hair to his cottage.

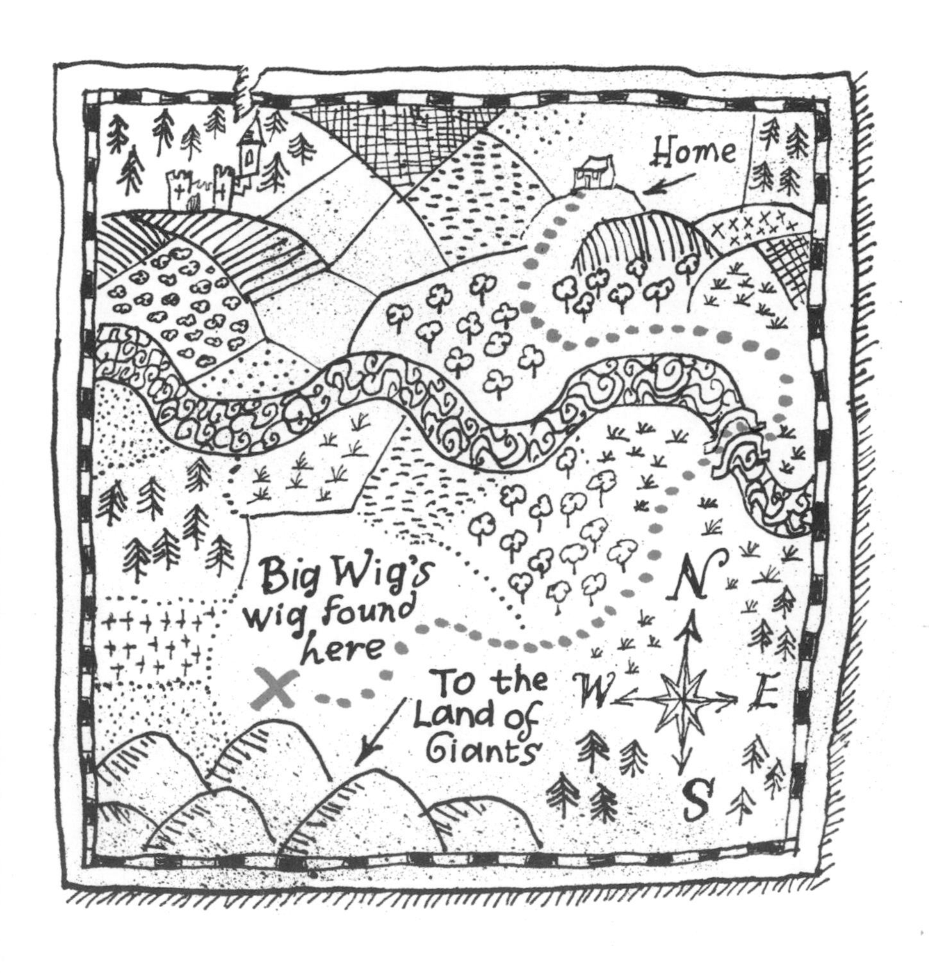

Jonathan's journey

His parents were delighted. They nailed it to their roof that very afternoon.

And everyone agreed it was the snazziest thatch in the land.

Chapter Three

Meanwhile Big Wig sat at home and sulked. He looked in the mirror and decided something must be done.

Then he had an idea.

Big Wig fetched his binoculars and went to look for his lost wig. He sat on a mountain and viewed the landscape.

He scanned every nook and cranny ...

and every crook and nanny ...

but he couldn't see his wig.

He was about to give up when ... suddenly he SPOTTED IT!

Now all he had to do was get it back. But that, alas, was easier said than done.

For Big Wig was a giant who was as timid as a mouse. He was as terrified of little folk as they were of giants!

So Big Wig spent a whole week at home chewing up pencils and thinking.

On Saturday, when all was dark, he crept to the edge of the Land of Giants.

He tiptoed over mountains (which were more like molehills to him) ...

and over lakes (which were more like puddles) ...

until he saw the cottage.

Big Wig crouched behind a tree.
He took a deep breath and blew
with all his might.

The cottage began to quake and quiver. The thatch began to shake and shiver. But it didn't budge an inch.

Jonathan and
his family stirred
in their beds.

But they soon went back to sleep.
Big Wig's plan hadn't worked.

He sloped off home even more miserable than before. But as he lit the fire, he had another idea.

Chapter Four

The next night Big Wig followed the track to the cottage. He held the bellows aloft and pumped away with all his strength.

Jonathan's family woke up as pictures fell off the walls and crockery crashed to the floor.

But the thatch on top of their house didn't shift at all.

Eventually they went back to bed, and were soon sleeping peacefully again.

Chapter Five

Big Wig was broken-hearted. The other giants teased him more than ever.

Big Wig hid indoors and moped.

After a whole month
he'd eaten all his food.
The only thing left
in the larder was
the pepper pot!

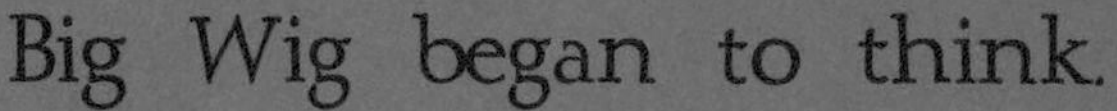

Big Wig began to think.

That night, armed with his pepper pot, Big Wig crept out of his house again. But before long he saw the bulky shape of Toothy Peg in the distance.

Toothy Peg was getting nearer! Big Wig tried to cover his bald head... Oops! The top came off the pepper pot.

Toothy Peg was very near now. Big Wig's nose tickled and twitched. Until...

He sneezed a giant sneeze.

Now Toothy Peg's nose began to twitch too and she sneezed an even bigger sneeze.

And then...

Toothy Peg's false teeth came flying out!

She stood there toothless as a toad.
"No one's perfect!" she grinned.
"That's true!" nodded Big Wig.

Soon they realized they had lots in common. They didn't mind jokes about being bald and toothless.

And because they didn't mind, the other giants soon grew tired of making jokes.

So, Big Wig and Toothy Peg lived happily hairless and toothless for the rest of their long lives.

And as for Toothy Peg's false teeth?

They're still standing today!

Walker Starters

The Dragon Test by June Crebbin, illustrated by Polly Dunbar
0-7445-9018-3
Hal the Highwayman by June Crebbin, illustrated by Polly Dunbar
0-7445-9019-1
Cup Run by Martin Waddell, illustrated by Russell Ayto
0-7445-9026-4
Going Up! by Martin Waddell, illustrated by Russell Ayto
0-7445-9027-2
Big Wig by Colin West
0-7445-9017-5
Percy the Pink by Colin West
0-7445-9054-X

Series consultant: Jill Bennett, author of
Learning to Read with Picture Books

First published 2003 by
Walker Books Ltd
87 Vauxhall Walk
London SE11 5HJ

10 9 8 7 6 5 4 3 2

This book has been typeset in
Alpha Normal, Calligraphic 810,
Calligraphic Antique Helvetica,
and M Garamond

Handlettering by Colin West

Printed in Hong Kong

British Library Cataloguing in Publication Data:
a catalogue record for this book is available
from the British Library

ISBN 0-7445-9017-5